Koda's Story

by Kay Barnham

PUFFIN BOOKS

PUFFIN BOOKS

Published by the Penguin Group
Penguin Books Ltd, 80 Strand, London WC2R 0RL, England
Penguin Putnam Inc., 375 Hudson Street, New York, New York 10014, USA
Penguin Books Australia Ltd, 250 Camberwell Road, Camberwell, Victoria 3124, Australia
Penguin Books Canada Ltd, 10 Alcorn Avenue, Toronto, Ontario, Canada M4V 3B2
Penguin Books India (P) Ltd, 11 Community Centre, Panchsheel Park, New Delhi – 110 017, India
Penguin Books (NZ) Ltd, Cnr Rosedale and Airborne Roads, Albany, Auckland, New Zealand
Penguin Books (South Africa) (Pty) Ltd, 24 Sturdee Avenue, Rosebank 2196, South Africa

Penguin Books Ltd, Registered Offices: 80 Strand, London WC2R 0RL, England

www.penguin.com

First published 2003
1

Set in 16 on 24pt Berkeley Book

Made and printed in England by Clays Ltd, St Ives plc

British Library Cataloguing in Publication Data
A CIP catalogue record for this book is available from the British Library

ISBN 0–141–31770–1

Contents

Chapter One

At the top of the world, the night sky is sometimes filled with ribbons of colourful light – light that swirls and whirls, dances and sways. This magical display is known as the Northern Lights.

Many years ago, wise people told that the lights were the spirits of those who had died. It was said that these spirits had the power to make changes in the world.

Once, there was a fight between a young man and a bear. The man died and *joined the spirits in the sky. But the man's two brothers wanted revenge. The younger brother chased the bear and killed her – leaving a baby bear without a mother.*

The spirits wanted to teach the man that it was wrong to kill, so they turned him into a bear. He was called Kenai. To change from a bear back into a man, Kenai had to prove to the spirits that he knew how to love all creatures ...

Koda chuckled to himself. It wasn't every day that he saw an enormous grizzly bear hanging upside-down in a tree. Bears were usually so careful – *they* didn't get caught in traps. Koda was only a bear cub – and he had never been caught. But this bear was well and truly trapped. He was dangling by one leg, swinging helplessly to and fro, looking as if he'd never be able to untie himself.

Suddenly, Koda had a brilliant idea. If he could free the grizzly then he'd have some company and if he had some company then . . .

Once he was sure there was no danger of hunters, Koda strolled out to meet the bear. 'How ya doin'?' he called.

The big grizzly spun round on the rope, slammed into the tree trunk and stared goggle-eyed at Koda.

'Guess you didn't see the trap, huh?' said Koda. 'I saw it from a mile away. You must be pretty embarrassed!' He lowered his voice to a whisper. 'Don't worry,' he said. 'I won't tell anyone.'

'What?' groaned the upside-down bear.

'You need to get down,' explained Koda slowly. 'Let me help.' He picked up a stick and swung it at the grizzly. *Smack! Smack! SMACK!*

'Oh . . . wait, wait, wait!' yelled the bear.

'Hold still!' Koda shouted back – and carried on smacking with his stick.

'Ow! No! Just . . . Ow! Stop that! Oof!' the grizzly yelled.

Koda stopped. 'It's no use,' he sighed. 'The only way to get down is to chew your own foot off.'

The trapped bear looked horrified. 'I don't need some stupid bear's help!' he roared. 'I just need the stick!'

'OK,' said Koda, laying the stick back

down on the ground.

The grizzly grabbed the stick and hoisted himself upwards to where the rope was tied. With a tug and a twist and a bite and a poke, he tried to loosen the rope that was holding him tight until . . .

'Arggh!' The bear swung downwards and thudded into the tree trunk.

'That was funny – do it again!' Koda giggled.

'Don't you have someplace to go?' muttered the bear.

'Yeah, the Salmon Run!' said Koda at once, grinning. Everything was going exactly to plan. 'How about this?' he said brightly. 'I get you down, then we go together. Deal?'

'Yeah, OK, fine,' agreed the grizzly. 'If you can magically get me down, I'll go with you to this . . . this . . .'

'Salmon Run,' Koda said.

'Whatever,' the bear sighed.

'You swear?' said Koda, just to be sure.

'Yeah, sure, fine,' agreed the bear. 'But this is a human trap. And you're just a dumb little bear . . . so there's really no way you're gonna be able to –'

Dink! Koda gently tapped a wooden peg out of the ground.

'– Arggh!' The great big grizzly was flung up into the air, before thumping back down to the ground. He was free!

Koda was delighted. His plan had worked perfectly. 'OK,' he announced, 'so what I was thinking is we travel by

day and sleep by night. My bedtime
is an hour after sunset, but I think
we'll –'

Then the little bear froze. A dangerous
scent was wafting along in the breeze.
'Run!' Koda shouted.

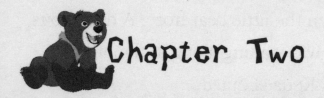# Chapter Two

From a distance, Koda watched as a dark shadowy figure appeared. It was a man – and he was carrying a deadly spear. Koda shivered, then stared in horror as he saw his new friend, Kenai, stumbling towards the man.

As if in slow motion, the man lifted his spear high above his head, ready to attack. 'Arrrgh!' he bellowed, throwing the spear at the towering grizzly.

It was time for Koda to get out of

there. He sped away towards the nearby glacier – a huge, frozen river of ice. Then he hurled himself through a gap leading into an icy cave. Seconds later, the big bear slid in after him.

'Is he gone?' whispered Koda.

'Shhhh!' hushed Kenai, clamping a large, furry hand over Koda's mouth.

A shadow fell over the chilly cave. The hunter could be seen through the icy ceiling, as he stood above them on the glacier. Then, after an endless pause, the man spun round – and left.

'Hello!' Koda quietly choked. 'I . . . can't . . . breathe!'

Kenai let go of Koda and sighed. 'Why's he chasing me?' he asked himself wearily.

'That's what they do,' replied Koda. His new friend really didn't seem to understand how humans and bears treated each other. 'It's lucky for him he didn't find us,' continued Koda, 'cos when I get in a fight I go all *craaaaazy*, and I'm a raging ball of brown fur! I mean . . . I don't wanna brag or nothing, but I've got some moves.'

'Oh, really?' said Kenai in a bored voice.

'Yep,' said Koda. And he showed the grizzly his very best attack movements – the Slasher and the Flying Fury of Death. 'The next time we run into that hunter …' he said in his scariest voice.

'There is no "we", OK?' grunted the bear. 'I'm not taking you to any

Salmon Run.'

'But you promised!' spluttered Koda. He couldn't believe it. They'd had a deal!

'Yeah, well, things change . . . See ya, kid,' Kenai said quietly, turning to go.

'Wait!' said Koda. He sighed. He didn't know why his big friend was miserable, but now was the time to tell him why he wanted them to stay together. 'The truth is – I got separated from my mother. And now, with this hunter around . . .'

'Kid, I've got my own problems,' said Kenai glumly.

'Come on, please?' pleaded Koda. 'Can't we just go together? There's a lot of bears and a ton of fish, and every night we watch the lights that touch the mountain. And last year Bucky found a –'

The grizzly suddenly looked up. 'What did you just say?' he asked.

'There's lots of bears and tonnes of fish –'

'No . . . the lights that touch the earth?'

'Yeah, they're at the top of the mountain, right by the Salmon Run,' said Koda, brightening up. He had no idea why his new friend wanted to see the magical lights that swirled around the sky, but at least it meant they could stay together after all!

'You're sure you can take me to where the lights touch the earth?' asked Kenai.

'Yeah,' said Koda. 'No problem!'

'All right,' agreed Kenai at last. 'We

leave first thing tomorrow.'

Koda sighed with happiness. His new friend would keep him safe until he found his mother. He curled up to sleep beside the big, grumpy, grizzly bear.

'And keep all that cuddly bear stuff to a minimum, OK, kid?' mumbled Kenai, pushing him away.

'My name's not kid. It's Koda,' said Koda. 'What's your name?'

The larger bear grunted in reply.

As they slept, coloured ribbons of light swirled outside, glowing through the icy walls of the glacier.

Chapter Three

The morning sun glinted off the glistening surface of the glacier. The hunter crept up to the crack in the ice and disappeared inside. Slowly, quietly, he slid between the frozen walls. Nothing would stop him from catching that grizzly bear . . .

The man took a deep breath, grasped his spear and jumped into the icy cave.

But the cave was empty.

*

Meanwhile, Koda had spotted the bendy, shiny, icy side of the glacier cave. Now he was going to have some fun!

Jumping to his feet, Koda made face after face in front of the wibbly-wobbly wall. He pulled his face this way and that, snorting with laughter at his reflection in the icy mirror.

'Yeah, cute,' drawled Kenai. 'Hey, I've got a mountain to get to. Come on, kid.'

Koda frowned. 'I told you before,' he said. 'My name's Koda. Say it with me. KO–DA.'

But the grizzly was bored of waiting. 'Sure your mother didn't ditch you, KO–DA?' he snapped.

'Actually, if you really want to know

how me and my mother got separated
. . .' he began, as they made their way
across a field, 'I was saving this story
for the Salmon Run, but I'll tell you.'
Koda paused dramatically. 'It was
probably the fifth or sixth most coldest
day in my entire life –'

'Oh, this sounds good,' interrupted
the bear. 'You should *definitely* save it.'

'You think so?' asked Koda.

Kenai nodded. 'Oh, yeah, for your
friends.'

'Oh,' said Koda. Then he had an
idea. 'Well, I have this other story . . .'

'Tell you what,' said Kenai rudely,
'how about no talking?'

'OK,' Koda said, thinking quickly.
'Then I'll sing!'

'No, no, no, no . . .' spluttered the grizzly.

But Koda had already burst into song. He sang about everything that was making him happy. He was on his way to the mountains. He was off to see new places, off to meet new friends. He would sleep under the stars, with the moon keeping watch over them.

He was heading towards the Salmon Run. And his new friend was coming with him.

 # Chapter Four

The mammoths trudged along, carrying the two bears on their long journey to the mountain top. As the mighty beasts walked, Koda jumped back and forth between their tusks, chattering non-stop. He'd never dreamt it would be so much fun to hitch a ride on a mammoth.

'Last year at the Salmon Run, my friend Bucky totally dared me to lick an iceberg. But I'd heard about this other cub that stuck his tongue to an iceberg. And then he started to float away. And so to save him they had to rip off his tongue. And now he "hath to talkth like thith" all the time. And –'

'Do you ever stop talking?' asked Kenai, pinching Koda's mouth shut.

Koda scrambled to the end of the mammoth's tusk. 'Ooooh! Look!' he shouted. 'The night rainbow! You can see the spirits from here . . .'

Kenai looked at Koda in surprise. 'You know about the Great Spirits?' he asked, as he watched the beautiful lights dance across the night sky.

'Yeah,' sighed Koda, wondering why his friend had such a weird look on his face. 'My grandma's up there – and my grandad. Mum says the spirits make all the magical changes in the world. Like how the leaves change colour or the moon changes shape or tadpoles change into frogs –'

'Yeah, I get it,' growled the big bear. 'You know, just for a *change*, maybe they could just leave things alone.'

'What do you mean?' asked Koda.

'My brother's a spirit.' Kenai sighed. 'And if it weren't for him, I ... I wouldn't be here.'

'You have a brother up there?' said Koda. 'What happened to him?'

'He was killed by a b–,' Kenai paused, 'by a monster.'

'What's your brother's name?' Koda asked.

'Sitka,' the bear replied.

Koda looked up at the lights above. 'Thanks, Sitka,' he said. 'If it weren't for you, I would've never met Kenai.' He snuggled up to the big bear – who actually let him stay there, for once. 'I always wanted a brother,' he murmured.

Huddled together on the back of a swaying mammoth, the big bear and the small bear looked up at the swirling patterns in the sky above. Soon, both bears were fast asleep.

Koda was dreaming – and it was a lovely dream. His mother was there with him and Kenai, who was his new big brother, and together they made one big, happy bear family, watching the colourful lights from the mountain top.

Suddenly, he felt a small nudge, a gentle shove and then a firm poke.

'Koda . . . Koda, come on. Koda, wake up!' said a deep voice.

'. . . two more months, Mum . . .' muttered Koda, his eyelids fluttering open to see Kenai staring down at him.

'So, where are we?' the grizzly asked.

Koda rubbed his eyes firmly and looked to the right. He saw rough, rocky ground. He looked to the left – rough, rocky ground. He looked straight ahead and behind. Guess what? Rough, rocky ground, too. Koda sighed. They were lost.

'Well, which way? Kenai asked. Looking crossly at Koda, he sprang off the mammoth.

'Hey! Riding mammoths was your idea!' said Koda, leaping to the ground, too. 'Thanks for the ride, guys,' he called to the mammoths. 'See ya!'

Koda plodded after the big grizzly bear.

# Chapter Five

'I'm sorry we're lost, OK?' said Koda. 'Even though it is pretty much your fault,' he added under his breath.

'*My* fault?' asked Kenai in disbelief.

'Just remember, if it weren't for me, you'd still be hanging upside-down right now!' Koda yelled back.

'Yeah, well, better than being stuck in the middle of nowhere with you and your blabbering mouth!' growled the grizzly. '"I'm lost",' he continued, pretending to be Koda. "'I can't find my mummy. Will you take me to the Salmon Run?'" He looked down at the small bear. 'Why don't you just grow up?'

Koda felt hurt. 'Fine,' he said bravely. 'I'll just go on my own then.'

'Fine,' said Kenai. 'Go ahead.'

'Fine,' repeated Koda. Then he slowly walked away from Kenai.

Behind him, the big bear sighed, before hurrying after his little friend.

By now, Koda had reached a rocky ridge. Peeping over and under and round the rocks, the curious bear spotted a cave. But this was no ordinary cave. Beautiful paintings of animals covered the smooth rock walls.

Together, Koda and Kenai stared at a picture of a bear and a hunter armed with a sharp spear.

Koda shivered. 'Those monsters are really scary . . .' he whispered, '. . . especially with those sticks.'

Kenai was still. 'Come on,' he said quietly. 'Let's go.'

Some time later, with Koda perched high on Kenai's furry shoulders, the two bears reached a dark, gloomy forest.

'So, do you recognize anything yet?' asked Kenai. 'Or maybe you can't see past my fat head . . .'

Koda spluttered with laughter. The big grizzly had made a joke. He must be enjoying himself at last! 'Well, if you hunched your shoulders a little, it wouldn't seem so big,' said Koda, grinning.

'Oh, you mean like this?' asked Kenai, bunching up his shoulders. Koda wobbled from side to side, laughing loudly.

'Or like this?' Kenai wiggled his shoulders. 'How about this?'

Koda roared with laughter as he was flung about. He wasn't scared – he and Kenai were friends and he knew that the grizzly wouldn't let him fall.

Then the little bear looked around. 'Hey, wait a second,' he said. Koda walked down Kenai's face and slid to the ground. 'I know this place!' he announced, as he scampered up the nearest hill.

'You do?' asked Kenai eagerly.

'Yeah! The Salmon Run's not far,' said Koda. He stopped at the top of the hill, adding, 'We just have to go through here.'

The big grizzly clambered to the hilltop and stared.

Below them lay a huge valley filled with bubbling mud pits and steaming yellow pools. Fountains of boiling water spurted into the air and lava explosions rocked the ground. Jagged cliffs towered on either side.

'Guess you didn't see the trap, huh?' said Koda
with a grin.

'Run!' Koda shouted.

'If it weren't for your brother, I would never have met you,' said Koda.

'Those monsters are really scary!' whispered Koda.

'Aaaiaaugh!' yelled Kenai. It wasn't a rock, but another bear!

'Every bear belongs here!' said Tug.

The Salmon Run is the biggest
party of the year!

'What do you expect from a little brother?'
Koda said, as Kenai ruffled his fur.

Koda was enjoying himself.
'And then out of the trees jumps the hunter!'

'Your mother's not coming,' Kenai whispered.

Koda turned and fled into the snowy distance.

It was the hunter, his eyes blazing.

Koda loved the man as much as he loved
the bear.

 **Chapter Six**

'Follow me!' shouted Koda cheerily.
He ran ahead, dodging about the
bubbling, spitting floor of the valley.

Crunch! Koda's foot broke through
the crust of earth.

Whoosh! A burst of steam shot up
into the air, hiding the little bear.

'Koda!' called Kenai, desperately
looking all around. 'Where are you?'

'Yaaaaah!' said Koda, leaping out
from behind him. He laughed and

laughed. Kenai's face had looked so funny!

'Don't do that!' growled Kenai angrily. But he looked very relieved to see Koda again.

The smaller bear chuckled. 'Scared you, didn't I?'

Kenai looked serious. 'There's *scared* and then there's *surprised*,' he said slowly.

'And you were both!' Koda chuckled.

The big grizzly was silent for a moment. Then he leant towards Koda, opened his enormous mouth and roared, 'Blaaaaaaah!'

Koda blinked and grinned. 'Nice try,' he said. But then he stopped smiling and began to tremble with fear.

'Kenai . . .' he gasped.

'You're not getting me this time,' Kenai said, chuckling.

Koda's eyes opened wider as he looked behind Kenai. His knees knocked together. 'No, Kenai – look out!' he shouted, and started to back away.

Thwack! A deadly spear stuck in the ground, right next to Kenai.

The big grizzly whirled round and saw the hunter. 'No . . .' he said quietly.

The man moved closer.

Koda looked at the hunter and Kenai. What was going on? This wasn't the time to stop and chat. It was time to run! 'Come on!' he shouted, zigzagging between muddy pools and hot fountains. 'Kenai, what are you waiting for?' Koda squinted across the valley floor. At last, he spotted his friend racing towards him. Koda gave a huge sigh of relief – until he saw the hunter who was closing in on him. Now *he* was in danger!

But, seconds later, Kenai grabbed Koda by the scruff of his neck and picked him up. Back across the valley they went, then on to a log bridge perched high above a rushing, churning river. They had nearly reached the safety of the other side of the gorge when Koda saw a dreadful sight.

The hunter was hacking away at the other end of the bridge with his spear. If he succeeded, Koda and Kenai would *faaaaall* . . .

By clinging on with his claws, the
big grizzly hung from the broken
bridge. Kenai flung Koda to safety,
before slowly dragging himself up,
paw over paw.

The two bears watched in horror as
the hunter gathered his strength and
attempted a giant leap across the gorge
to where they were standing. He
nearly made it. But, instead, landed
on the dangling log bridge. The
remains of the bridge couldn't take his
weight. The log broke free from the
ledge, then plunged down, down,
down . . .

Kenai was frozen to the spot, staring
into the raging river far below.

Koda wondered why the big grizzly

was sad. Kenai looked like he'd lost a member of his family, instead of a hunter who had wanted to kill them. What was wrong with him?

Then the man's head popped above the water's surface – he was alive.

# Chapter Seven

After the encounter with the hunter,
Koda was thoughtful for a long time.
'Why do they hate us, Kenai?' he
finally said, as the two bears walked
through a dark forest.

'We're bears,' explained Kenai.

'So?' replied Koda.

'So . . . you know how bears are,'
Kenai said. 'They're . . . they're killers.'

Koda was confused. 'What?
Which bears? I'm not like that and

you're not like that.'

'Well, obviously not *all* bears,' the big grizzly said quickly. 'I mean, you're OK. But most bears . . . most bears will look for any excuse to attack a human.'

Now Koda was really confused. 'But Kenai, *he* attacked us.'

'You know,' mumbled Kenai, tripping over a tree root, 'you're just . . . you're just a cub. When you're older, you'll understand –'

Suddenly, a noisy seagull interrupted Kenai. 'Fish! Fish!' the bird squawked.

'Huh?' said Kenai.

Koda laughed with delight. 'We made it!' he shouted. 'We're here! Come on!'

'Fish! Fish! Fish! Fish!' cried more

seagulls, swooping towards them.

'Hey, get away from me!' yelled Kenai. 'Go on – shoo!' The big grizzly stumbled backwards through the trees. He tripped over a rock and . . .

Splosh! Kenai fell into the river. He bobbed to the surface, gasping and spluttering, and grabbed on to a nearby rock. Then the rock began to move . . . It wasn't a rock at all – it was another bear!

'Aaaugh!' hollered Kenai. 'Auaghggh!' He slowly opened his eyes. 'Aa . . . ah . . . ah . . . a . . . ah?'

'Hey, you're stirring up the water, dude,' said a huge grizzly bear that was even bigger than Kenai.

'Yeah, try not to scare off the fish

there, buddy,' added a different bear.

Koda was surprised. It was as if Kenai had never sat in a river surrounded by grizzly bears before – he looked terrified. Then Koda noticed one of his old friends sitting on the river bank beside a pile of fish. 'Tug!' he shouted.

'Hey, Koda!' replied Tug. 'Come here! Look at you!'

'Hey, Tug!' said Koda. 'Have you seen my mum yet?'

Tug looked thoughtful. 'No, as a matter of fact, I haven't seen her.'

'Ha!' Koda said. 'Me and my friend, Kenai, got here first!'

'He's with you?' asked Tug.

Kenai waved nervously. 'Uh, hi,' he said.

'I've never seen you at the Salmon Run before,' said Tug. 'Where are you from?'

'Er . . . uh . . . I . . .' stammered Kenai.

'And, see, Kenai?!' exclaimed Koda, pointing upwards. 'There's the mountain, just like I promised. And the lights touch the top every single night . . .'

Kenai looked.

'It's going to be a lot harder getting up there than it was riding those mammoths,' said Koda with a grimace.

'Mammoths?' asked the other bears.

'That's kind of weird,' added Tug.

'Yeah, he does a lot of weird stuff,' said Koda brightly. 'He's never even sharpened his claws on a tree . . . He's never hibernated before . . . He doesn't know how to lick himself clean . . .'

Kenai rushed forwards. 'Koda! Koda!' he said, clamping a hand over the cub's mouth. 'Can I talk to you for a second?' he asked quietly. Kenai sat down on the shore. 'OK, Koda, I . . . uh . . . I gotta get going.'

Koda grinned at his friend. 'Well, when you come back we can go and –'

'I . . . I won't be coming back,' said Kenai.

Koda couldn't believe his ears. 'What? Why not?' he asked in a trembling voice.

Kenai screwed his face up. 'Because . . . well, it's a little hard to explain,' he mumbled.

'You're leaving?' asked Tug.

'Ah . . . Well, I uh . . . I mean, yes,' said Kenai, his words tripping over each other. 'It's just that . . . I don't belong here.'

Tug towered above Kenai and Koda. 'Don't belong?' he boomed. 'Every bear belongs here!'

Koda grinned. Tug would persuade his friend to stay.

'Listen,' said Tug. 'We care for each other and share with each other. We're one big, happy family. You're a bear too – we'd like to welcome you to our festival.'

Kenai nodded slowly.

And Koda grinned happily.

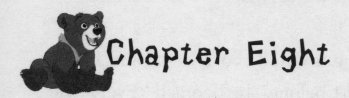# Chapter Eight

Koda was contented. He'd had a great day fishing with Kenai and now it was storytelling time – Koda's favourite part of the Salmon Run. One by one, each bear told the others about the most exciting thing that happened to them that year. Tug went first. He'd felled a mighty tree that was blocking the view from his cave. Now the family of chipmunks that had been living in the tree were staying at his place.

Tug got ready to throw the storytelling fish to the next bear. 'All right, everybody! Come on – let's see some paws in the air. Who's gonna be next?'

'Pick me!' called Koda. He wanted to tell the story of how he and his mother had been separated. Perhaps someone would know where to find her.

But Koda missed the fish and Kenai caught it instead. 'Here you go, Koda,' he said, handing the fish to the little bear.

'You've got to tell it,' said Koda.

'That's right, Kenai,' agreed Tug. 'You caught it, you tell it.'

'All right!' said Kenai. 'This year, I went on the longest, hardest, most exhausting journey I've ever been on – with the biggest pain in the neck

I've ever met.'

Koda looked at him sadly.

'But,' added Kenai, ruffling Koda's fur, 'what do you expect from a little brother?'

Koda grinned from furry ear to furry ear.

'OK, buddy,' said Kenai, tossing him the fish. 'Your turn.'

'OK, here we go!' began Koda, clearing his throat. 'It was probably the fifth or sixth most coldest day in my entire life. Me and Mum were eating fish and having a great time when, all of a sudden, she pushes me into the bushes and tells me to be real quiet.' He lowered his voice. 'There was something in the woods running right towards us . . . getting closer . . . and closer . . . and then out of the trees jumps . . . *a hunter*!'

Kenai gasped.

'And now there's nowhere for Mum to go,' Koda went on. 'The monster has her backed up against this giant glacier!' Koda was really enjoying himself now. This was a very good story. He took a deep breath. 'And they were all round her, poking her with sticks. Then the whole glacier broke! Mum and the monster fell into the water – there was ice everywhere! Then the monster disappeared beneath the water . . .'

'Hey, Koda,' asked one of the bears, 'so what happened next? Was she OK?'

'Oh, yeah,' said Koda proudly. 'It

takes more than that to stop my mum. She got out of the water OK. But that's when we got separated. Some other monsters burst through the trees and she went to protect me from them. Not long after that, I met Kenai.' Koda turned round to look at his friend.

But Kenai had vanished!

Chapter Nine

Koda couldn't sleep. He spent the whole night wondering where Kenai had got to and if he was coming back. When the morning finally arrived he set off to find his friend.

Finally, he spotted him lying down just over a mountain ridge. Koda crept over the ridge, moving silently forwards. Then he sprung on to Kenai's furry back with a 'Raaaaaaarrrr!'

'Scared you again, huh?' said Koda.

'Yeah,' replied Kenai in a miserable voice.

'Where have you been?' asked Koda. His friend didn't look at all well. 'You look horrible,' he said. 'My mum says that if you eat too much fish, you should just lie down.'

'Koda . . .' mumbled Kenai, as the little bear jumped around him. 'There's something I need to tell you . . . You know that story you told last night?'

Koda nodded.

'Well,' continued Kenai, 'I have a story to tell you . . .'

'Really?' asked Koda, picking berries off a nearby bush. 'What's it about?'

'Well, it's kind of about a man and kind of about a bear . . . But mostly it's about a monster,' explained Kenai.

Koda sat down quietly beside his friend and waited for him to begin.

'Once,' said Kenai softly, 'there was a fight between a man and a bear. The man died and joined the spirits in the sky. But the man's two brothers wanted revenge. The younger brother chased the bear and killed her – leaving a baby bear without a mother.' Kenai hung his head in shame. 'Your mother's not coming,' he whispered to Koda.

'No . . . no . . .!' Koda wept, his eyes filling with salty tears. Who was this man – this monster – that had killed his mother . . .?

But Kenai hadn't finished telling his story. 'The spirits wanted to teach the man that it was wrong to kill,' he continued, 'so they turned him into a bear. To change back into a man, the bear had to prove to the spirits that he knew how to love all creatures . . .'

Koda stared in disbelief, leaping away from the big grizzly as if he'd been scalded. No wonder he didn't know how to act like a bear – Kenai was a man! Worst of all, Kenai had killed his mother!

'I'm sorry, Koda,' said Kenai, his face full of sadness. 'I'm so sorry.'

Koda turned and fled into the snowy distance.

Sometime later, Koda returned.

He looked sadly at the big footprints

that led through the snow and up the steep slopes of the great mountain. So that was where Kenai had gone.

Koda didn't know what to think about Kenai's story, but he did know that he had to find his friend. He had to give him the chance to explain. The little bear took a deep breath and set off.

Chapter Ten

Koda trudged onwards and upwards.
The wind was biting and snowflakes
swirled all around him. Soon, he was
chilled right through. But he kept on
walking, right to the top of the great
mountain and over the ridge until –

'Aaaaahhh!'

The hunter was standing over Kenai,
his eyes blazing.

'Denahi, please . . .' groaned Kenai.

The hunter raised his knife high

above his head.

Without a second thought, Koda hurtled towards Denahi. *Bam!* He slammed into the hunter, knocking him away from Kenai.

'Koda . . .?' said Kenai softly.

But there wasn't time to talk. Now the hunter was chasing Koda.

The grizzly rushed forwards to save his little friend, but at that very moment, a large, glowing eagle swooped out of the sky, grasped Kenai with its mighty talons and lifted him into the air.

Koda and the hunter watched in astonishment as magical energy whirled round the bear. The eagle slowly lowered Kenai to the ground . . . once again in the form of a man.

Kenai reached out towards Koda, saying human words that the little bear could not understand.

But Koda didn't need to know the meaning of the words. He looked into Kenai's eyes and knew that he loved this man as much as he'd loved the bear. He ran towards Kenai, jumped and landed in his arms.

Kenai hugged the little bear tightly. Then he looked towards the hunter and at the great eagle. All at once, his face seemed happy, sad – and full of love.

Koda remembered the story that Kenai had told him. *To change back into a man, the bear had to prove to the spirits*

that he knew how to love all creatures . . .
Kenai had proved that he loved both
men and bears, so he had turned back
into a man. Koda was pleased, but sad
at the same time. He had lost his
brother, the bear.

Or had he . . .?

Kenai nodded to the hunter and the
eagle, speaking the strange language of
humans. Then slowly, wonderfully,
magically, he changed back into the
grizzly bear that Koda knew and
loved.

'Kenai!' shouted Koda joyfully.

Kenai had made his choice. He'd
chosen to become a bear and stay with
Koda. The little bear had his very own
brother, at last.

Above them, ribbons of colourful light swirled and whirled, danced and swayed in the night sky.

And then vanished.

Help us to help our friends

Animals around the world need your help. Every day we are losing forests, rivers and other areas that animals need to live in. WWF is a charity working to protect wild animals and wild places. You can help them best like this:

- Ask your parent or guardian to support WWF for as little as £2 per month
- Ask your parent or guardian to adopt an animal with WWF for as little as £2 per month
- Organise a fun event, at school or at home, to raise money for WWF

Thank you

Koda pledge for WWF

Yes, I want to help wildlife, please send me:

❑ Information about becoming a WWF supporter to show my parent/guardian (I01)
❑ Information about adopting an animal (panda, dolphin, orang utan, tiger, elephant, rhino) to show my parent/guardian (541)
❑ A free fundraising pack to help me organise my own event to raise money for WWF (I11)

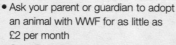

My first name is: _____ My surname is: _____

My address is: _____

_____

My postcode is: _____ My date of birth is: _____

After getting permission from your parent/guardian, please post this coupon to us for your FREE information pack to be sent to you. Cut out this coupon and put it in an envelope and address it to: Brother Bear, FREEPOST SCE729, WWF-UK, Panda House, Weyside Park, Godalming, Surrey, GU7 1BR, UK.

Parent/Guardian: Your child will be added to WWF's mailing list and will receive occasional information about events and activities they can choose to participate in. We will never mail your child directly to ask for money. We will not pass your child's details to any organisation with whom we co-operate.

G150

Under the terms of the Data Protection Act 1988, you have the right to advise us at any time if you do not wish your child to receive further communications from WWF. You can advise us of this now by ticking this box ❑